BLUE

COLORS: CHAPTER II

TYLER VO

Internal illustrations by Emma Lin
Cover by Jenny Nguyen

Parental Advisory: Explicit Content (mature language and graphic content)

A very special thank you to Emma Lin and Jenny Nguyen for creating artwork to bring my visions to life. I adore and appreciate both of you.

I wish I could stop time and marvel indefinitely at the vastness of our world before either of us inevitably disintegrates.

Copyright © 2020 by Tyler Vo
All rights reserved. This book or any portion thereof may not be reproduced or used in any manner whatsoever without the express written permission of the publisher except for the use of brief quotations in a book review.

ISBN 979-8-5710-4652-7

Dear Reader,

Welcome to Chapter 4 of my life's personal story and Volume II of "Colors." To be able to say that I've published four (!!) books in five years is an incredible blessing that I will always very graciously cherish. Watching myself grow as a writer and become much more secure with my ideas as well as confident in my ability to transform and mature my creative boundaries has been especially humbling throughout this journey. Part of my desire to seriously pursue writing, besides philanthropy, was to prove to myself that I was more than just a morose poet with an extensive vocabulary. After writing an autobiography and publishing my first real poetry collection, I decided to allow myself to simply write without confining my works to any genre or style. This led me to turn a long withstanding idea buried deep in the far outer banks of my brain into reality: the "Colors" series. As someone who constantly has a plethora of unfinished and unpublished pieces just waiting for the "right" book to be included in, I used "Colors" to share more of my art with you guys that would otherwise never be read. "Colors" provided me with a unique and tasteful way to combine a lot of my ideas into one holistic and cohesive product. I know it hasn't been too long since I published "RED" but the overwhelmingly positive reception from you guys made me extremely motivated to write "BLUE."

Ever since I conceived the idea of writing the "Colors" series a few years ago, I was super excited for this particular volume. Blue is a color with which I've always identified, especially when I was younger. It was my favorite color for as long as I can remember, at least until I learned about more descriptive colors (periwinkle). I loved its tranquility and calming allure while also being a harbinger of a particular blend of loneliness and sadness. Because I personally associate blue with myself, this volume is very important to me. The topics I've written about in this book are much more sentimental to me and I think I've somehow become even more vulnerable and honest with you guys than ever before.

With this project specifically, my goal was to make the entire reading experience exude an overall sense of "blue" throughout. Because of that, there will not be any introductions before any of the chapters. Instead, you will see unique artwork created by some of my wonderful friends who have selflessly helped me bring my vision to fruition. I hope that you allow the artwork to guide you through the chapters and reflect on the thoughts that cross your mind when you look at the art. Unlike "RED," the order of the chapters in this book matter and I strongly recommend reading from start to finish as I've intended. My talented friends put a lot of effort and work into their contributions to this project and there is nothing more rewarding for me than to make my writing a communal product. My writing is extremely personal and my friends being my biggest supporters plays a huge part in that.

Once again, I am hoping that you will enjoy what I have to offer. There are so many things I want to tell the world and I will continue to give you all a piece of me with every poem, story, or narrative I print on these pages. As always, thank you for your support and patronage. This book would not exist without you.

-Tyler

LONELINESS
11

WATER
23

SLEEP
27

SKY
33

MUSIC
37

ALEXTTDO
87

Loneliness

deserving

i woke up thinking about dying this morning
this happens more often than i let on.
i'd rather not worry those around me;
they got enough going on.
it starts off very routine and nonchalant:
no ceremonies, no fireworks, no sirens
just a wistful desire to quiet the heavy sighs
knocking on my chest.
i quickly scan the room for something to
cut
asphyxiate
intoxicate
nothing.
so I climb out of bed and start my day.
today was no different than before
i silently cursed under my breath when my eyes
opened
to the gentle rings of light peeking out from overcast
skies
it's taxing, really, igniting and firing up one's body
to
produce
create
breathe
think
love
for a lotto's chance at making the grand exchange.
not to mention the exhaustive efforts invested in
attempting to avoid devolution into sheer insanity
through conversation and interaction,
many of which remain callously futile *alla fine*.

i find myself tip-toeing around landmines
unintentionally missing each one
even with steps paralleled only by a drunkard's
stumble

wondering why my cowardice reigns supreme
to my own heartfelt desires.
what is it that i could have possibly done
to be deserving of this?
of these magnificent travels and worldly possessions
the beauty of different time zones and cultures
these golden tickets to an increasingly better life.
what right does someone who never asked to be born,
with no appetite for life or animation and a burning self-hatred
have to any entitlement to your perfect love?
please stop wasting your precious affection
on someone who cares naught and deserves even less.
one of these days I'll either wake up or never again
regardless you'd be better off holding onto
that boundless adoration you so generously adorn unto others
i'd hate to watch you spill any more than you already have
on the corpse of what we used to be
while waiting for the resurrection of what should have been.

undeserving

The misery was almost contagious-
Sunken countenances built from empty souls
Floating sullenly across the black asphalt roads and cracked sidewalks.
The vibrantly bright lights of the city reflect poorly on empty faces.
As I walk through the densely packed alleyways and streets
I see isolation and reservation but no loneliness.
There was immense temptation to acquiesce to the total silence surrounding me:
The sounds that croaked from my withered cords were foreign
But the language of the world around me was horrifyingly unfamiliar too.
My voice kept my thoughts company in the quarantined confines of my head
And I slowly and gruelingly found comfort in my own soul.

After finishing my last undergraduate final exam ever, I sat in my friend's room and spontaneously decided to take a solo trip to Japan for two weeks. I booked flights and hotels three weeks beforehand and intentionally decided to forego any pre-made plans or itinerary. I had never traveled completely alone before and was equally excited and anxious about what the trip would bring. I was prioritizing relaxing, debriefing before starting my first post-grad job, and just soaking in the culture.

The previous ten or so months leading up to when I departed for Tokyo were some of the most emotionally and psychologically trying episodes of my life. It started early in 2019 with the most serious and intense suicidal phase I've ever survived.

The sharp and rapid opening of my eyes each morning
Brought a searing burn to my sleep-deprived, insomniac corneas
Straight through to my swirling brain and its badly beaten and bruised prefrontal cortex.
For breakfast I inhaled a new way to kill myself
And gave myself a few minutes to swallow before the insidiousness could manifest itself
Into driving my car off the side of a freeway on my way to work
Or overdosing on whatever I could find nearby
Or self-asphyxiation.

Nothing could prevent the thoughts from invading my conscience with their sinister manipulation and convenient spontaneity. Multiple times per day the unwelcomed neighbor kicked down the front door and tried selling me on life after death. There was nothing in particular I was holding onto but I felt my mind gradually wanting to relax my grip and succumb to whatever dark magnetism was drawing me closer and closer to self-actualized tragedy. Eventually, I became so engrossed in my own self-pity and disillusioned rejection of self that I correlated my inability to take my own life with the conclusion that I was truly undeserving of all the love and light in my life.

What ensued was a rather extreme attempt at forced loneliness in order to try and comprehend my emotions. I ended relationships, distanced friendships, and did my best to spend most of my time within my own head, undistracted, on an unguided journey to connect psychology with spirituality. I essentially went as off the grid as possible but only superficially. I was still finishing up my degree and working 30+ hours a week at my internship but outside of my obligations I tried to be completely isolated. This proved to be horribly detrimental to both my mental and physical health as my already catastrophically horrible (lack of) sleeping habits continued to worsen. For someone who had previously averaged an aggregate total of 4-5 hours of sleep per day since middle school and operated relatively normally despite, I obviously could not afford to lose much more sleep.

Most of my recurring memories from this time include episodes wherein I found myself staring blankly at the walls in my apartment for hours at a time and occasionally screaming into the empty recesses of my sweltering summer prison. As my sleep dwindled to a paltry average of 3-4 hours per night, I experienced blackouts and momentary extreme blood pressure drops with increasing regularity. I finally felt mortal. I had been living in continuous overdrive and borrowing energy from future reserves with no regard for human life and the weight of constantly telling myself I was still healthy and "this is just how I am" collapsed on my soul. I desperately needed help and I needed to change how I was treating my mind, body, and heart.

It's hard to recognize true freedom right away:
It slips inside your mind slowly and insidiously,
Creeping over your worries and absent obligations
Until one day it wakes you up from the first peaceful night in recent memory.
The morning air rings the alarm with a different scent than days past.
It smells oddly pleasant
Not quite sweet but there's no bitter taste from last night's decisions.
You climb out of bed and look around at a blank canvas

Eagerly awaiting its first strokes of the day,
Beckoning you towards its infinite void
But this null feeling is filled with a coalescence of colors, not darkness.
It's patient. Allowing you to take your time and measure your steps
Cautiously as you try to understand your newfound liberty.
There are no mistakes
No faults. No expectations.

Trapping myself in a foreign country for two weeks wherein I didn't speak the native language at all proved to be the counterintuitive mess I needed in order to understand myself and my emotions. The first couple of nights were horrid and honestly depressing, not to mention scary. I got lost on the subway and arrived at my hotel hours later than I planned to. On top of that, my first meal was a disaster. I dined at a local izakaya and nobody in the entire restaurant spoke a lick of English and the menu had no pictures or translations. When I got back to my hotel room that evening, the sudden reality of my situation dawned on me. What had I gotten myself into? I was so scared that the next two weeks would be merely an exhausting continuation of my first day.

When I awoke early the next morning, I immediately remembered the immense discomfort and uncertainty I fell asleep with and was initially too rattled to get up and start my day. I lay in bed for a while longer before housekeeping forced me to get up and leave for the daily cleaning. With no plans or itinerary on deck, I decided to go to a nearby park to people watch and read. I spent hours at that park, watching schoolchildren run and laugh with their classmates, admiring elderly folk strolling and taking in the crisp morning air, and reading my book. I only took one quick break to eat lunch at a popular ramen chain nearby which served meals in isolated booths to individual patrons. That entire day brushed by me akin to the biting winds that began to pick up at the park, ushering me back to the subway station to make my way back to my hotel.

I had another quiet night, knowing better than to revisit another local restaurant for dinner, and went to sleep early under a peaceful series of deep, calming breaths. I survived my first full day in Japan and knew moving forward that I had complete control over how my next two weeks went. The rest of my trip was breathtaking and emancipating. I met such wonderful people whose generosity I will always be indebted to and immersed myself in Japan's beautiful culture. While a bit forlorn that I couldn't stay longer, I came home with much less weight on my shoulders and much more appreciation for time spent completely alone.

It's a fear we try our hardest to avoid facing
Yet the more we desperately distance ourselves from its insidious fangs
The more painful its bite stings.
Our interactions are mostly fleeting
But distracted faces and bright screens merely keep us from
Waltzing with our own demons and vulnerabilities.
It's this inability to confront the repressed and suppressed
That are imprisoned internally within our heavy hearts and vapid souls
Which forces us to manically seek refuge in whichever
Comforting capacity opens its doors to us first.
We don't speak on our fear of loneliness
As if even uttering the words into the biosphere

Will release spores of a horrifying plague into our cushioned reality.
There exists a predilection of belief that we don't need to
Venture deep into our core and familiarize ourselves with our underlying insecurities and shortcomings:
That all still yet to be discovered we already knew.

I knew.
I had caught a glimpse of the opaque darkness that saturates my mind before.
It really wasn't an inviting place.
But for the better part of a year I dove straight into the eye of the storm,
Stripped bare of my inhibitions and fears,
Ready to understand why my mind and heart behaved the way they did so often.
I spiraled. Immensely. More than I had ever before.
I was suicidal. I drove myself mad.
I kept weighing my life on a balance to see if it was worthy of continuing.
My fears of failure and lack thereof of death haunted me ceaselessly
While I continued treading through uncharted headspace.
Perhaps it was the synthetically manufactured isolation I surrounded myself with
That prevented me from coming to grips with the fact that
My emotional and psychological aversion to loving myself
Stemmed from a long withstanding inability to comprehend love.
I wasn't truly alone. I was hardheadedly chasing loneliness at all times
And that was indeed what blinded me.

However, the Devil shows himself eventually if you spend enough time summoning him.

I met him face to face and stared into the hypnotic pools of his eyes
And saw a dark reflection of myself looking back at me,
A ghoulish, lifeless grin spread across its face.
Before I had enough time to react, my demonic counterpart lurched forward
With its outstretched arms and slashed its claws
Across my body through my hollow bones, exposing my rapidly beating heart.
The monster immediately ripped my heart out and
Dove headfirst into the cavity of my chest in an attempt to possess my body.
A violent clash between complacency and anxiety consumed my soul
As I erupted in a manic burst of emotional instability.

I woke up this morning to one of those piercing rays of sunlight that seem to sneak their way past a wall of foreboding clouds
And break through to the Earthly plane to provide a dash of brightness unto an otherwise bleak midsummer day.
The thin air from outside wafts through my nose and invigorates my awakening senses.
Life begins to slowly pump its way through my blood vessels as I begin my day:
undeserving of all the self-loathing and self-destructive thoughts
undeserving of the torturous repetition of receding twice as fast as proceeding
undeserving of constantly undermining my own happiness
undeserving of feeling shame for wanting to experience my own emotions
and finally deserving of love and peace within my soul.

Water

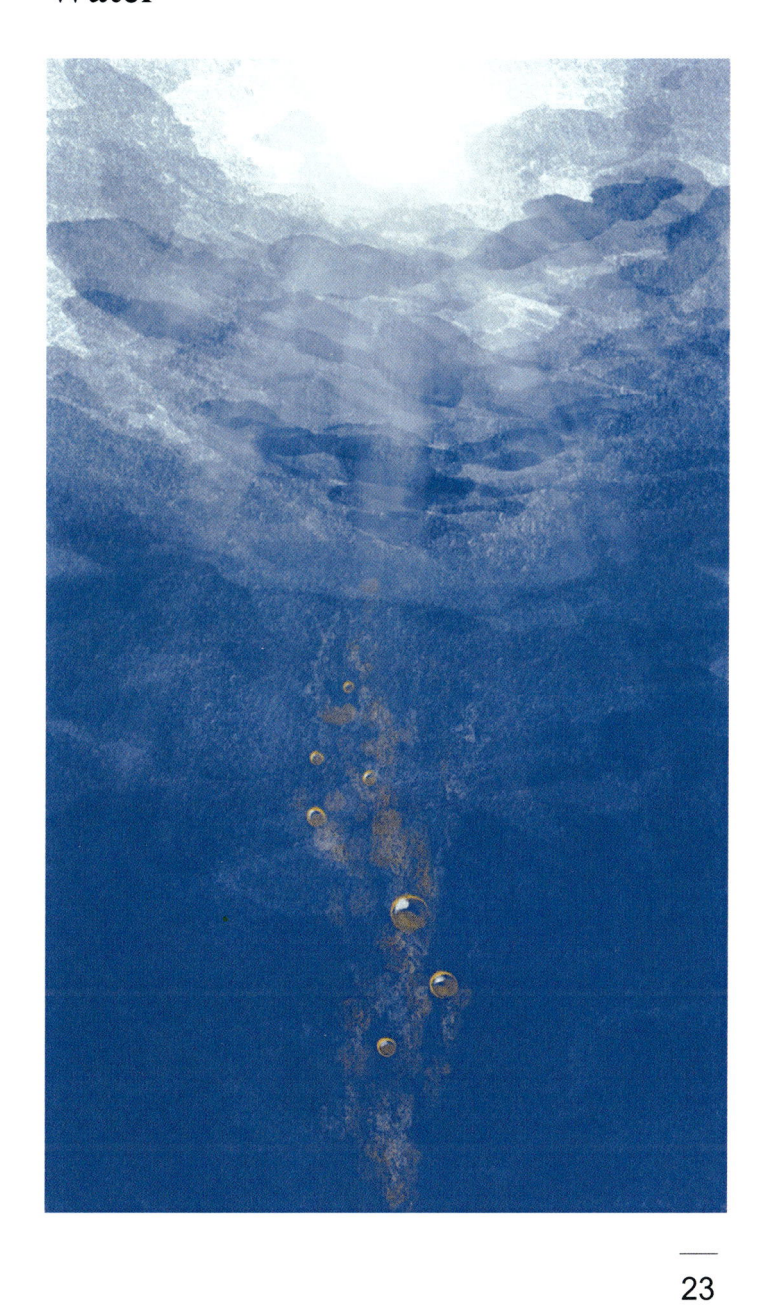

Drowning

Living with you is like a fever dream:
When you come around I feel everything at once,
The most intense conflagration of emotions
All entangling and passing through me simultaneously
And everything seems to just make sense.
Loving you is like a shooting star:
Incredibly beautiful and frustratingly fleeting.
When we're connected and together
There's an invincibility that runs through my spine
And an overwhelming sense of security and belonging
That vanishes instantaneously when you decide to walk away.
I wish I could have you forever without the tempest that follows.

I remember when we were younger you used to randomly push me away and disappear for months at a time
Oh, how I would stay up late, unable to fall asleep, wondering where you went.
When the blurry days and lonely nights would inevitably add up and weigh on my heart I began to unravel-
Questioning my self-worth and asking the walls in my room why you couldn't love me the way I needed you to.
Sometimes it seemed as if you knew I wanted to know peace but you kept the key tucked away somewhere hidden
Where only you could find it and dangled empty promises in front of me, dragging me along with you but always still just out of reach

And it hurt and kept hurting and still hurts to see you withhold the one piece of me I need left to feel authentic
All while not knowing the reasons behind your cruel intentions.

There's solace to be found in knowing who you are and why you are that allows you to transcend beyond trivial insecurities that blind and haunt and taunt and pull on your heels with every step forward but you,
You are a cancer that my bloodstream pathetically needs to live but your selfish attitude and whimsically fleeting generosity comes and goes whenever it suits you best and I can't keep sticking around sedentarily in one place while you explore the taste of the fruits of this world unbothered by the damage you've done to my sanity
Because I'm the one who deserves to be free from the chains you shackled me with and I deserve to be happy with myself when I wake up in the mornings and I deserve to love myself wholly and completely but you have taken that from me with reckless abandon and it never seems like you ever gave a shit about me no matter how many times you've said you needed me because I need you and every day feels like another lifetime in the deep end and the pressure is building insurmountably on my shoulders pressing me down further and further as the ocean floor continues to fall and disappear from view the murkiness and darkness of the abyss blend into one I can't see where I am anymore and my arms have stopped flailing and my legs won't kick anymore my body is just lifeless and floating I can't breathe my lungs have filled with water somebody please save me from myself I can't do this anymore how much longer

Sleep

In My Head

I had a dream about you a few years ago:
It was nothing special but I remember how noisy everything was.
We were standing on an overcrowded subway train
The heat was sweltering but it was nighttime
And there was a jovial crowd of drunk people all around us.
In every direction there were friends laughing hysterically and lovers gazing romantically
Voices clamored on top of each other until there was no more discernible dialogue left to hear-
Just a wave of noise constantly crashing into my headspace.
But when I tried to break through the plane of inebriation enveloping me
I caught your magnificent sapphire eyes at the other end of the train
Looking right through me and into my soul.
A sudden quiet swept through the platform and my eyes were rudely opened by the morning sun.

I had a dream about you a couple months ago:
On a bright Sunday morning we ran into each other at a café.
Well, actually, you bumped into me while turning around after picking up your coffee.
We both checked for any spills and then you looked up at me,
A nervous flush of red flooding your embarrassed cheeks
And a warm but quickly receding smile placed itself on your face.
Once again you stared into my eyes, wondering if you recognized me
But of course, we were never able to introduce ourselves the last time.

With a hurried apology, you grabbed your drink and sat down with some friends
How strange that you reappeared after all this time; I thought I had forgotten about you but I guess my mind just couldn't let you go.

I had a dream about you last night:
I found myself walking through a placid pasture purely illuminated by a soft glowing moonlight.
The songs of the sky twinkled above as a collection of speckled stars beamed overhead.
Peering around the meadow I felt a warm gust of wind rush through me
But the stalks of grass enveloping me barely experienced a ripple.
The night was calm and the air was mild:
Our heavenly temperaments had coalesced beautifully into the perfect ambience.
Once more, the wind brushed past my shoulder with gentle comfort
As I quickly turned to follow its contact.
Walking towards the direction I sensed the breeze traveled
I began to notice the world around me growing stiller and rigid.
Suddenly, I was no longer moving forward, but rather in place,
Staring down a tunnel of dark matter as the moon shut its light on me
And a bitter cloud of icy cold rained down over me.

Through all the chaos you always seemed to find me in my dreams:
I thought you were the remedy to my nightmares
But when the world seemed to be at peace around us
You led me straight into the cold, empty abyss,
Stranding me with the horrifyingly dark reality of my inhibitions.

They say the only faces you see in your dreams are real
So maybe one of these days I'll escape the tantalizing idea of you
And find out if we could be true
Because I can only have you be the girl of my dreams for so long.

Sky

what comes after this

Can we slow down for just a minute?
We have the rest of our lives to run and jump
Until we collapse to the Earth and marvel at the serenity of the spring sky,
Our hearts palpitating rapidly, sending our chests on a roller coaster
Up towards the warm light and back down onto the soft grass.
The motion of the clouds parting away from the sun is quite majestic.
When we're still, the world seems to revolve around us.
We can see episodes of our lives play out in front of us and the sky is our projector.
Let's just hit pause and take a look at where we are:
I want to keep us in the still frame I captured with my camera,
Frozen in a moment we'll undoubtedly forget in a few weeks
With the speckled shadows of trees towering over us
As we stood at the edge of a hillside path staring out at miles of wistful grasslands,
Your hand lightly clasped in mine.
I love how the wrinkles in your palm fit mine perfectly
As if our every crease and asymmetry was woven together and stitched commensurately
So together we could close the wounds, fill the voids, and cover our flaws
But this is just an infinitesimal cross section of our converging timelines.
You knew that.
Where do we go when I pull us out of the collections of pictures?
The ones oversaturated with smiles and carefully filtered backdrops?

We've both seen the ending to our movie
It doesn't last long beyond the beautiful scenes by the water and under the stars
But what if the director's cut could at least keep us entertained a while longer?
I can't change what happens to us or how we fell from grace and wonder.
I can only delay the inevitable and bring us back to the shots and individual thumbnails
From anniversaries and Christmases past
When we thought our love would never run out of time.
Our script was never intended to exceed the original run time
And so I practiced my farewells at the same time I overcame my fear of 'I love you'-s
It must have broken your heart to hear me tell you both
But I rehearsed for months as you slept silently next to me
So that I could refrain from crying and keep my voice steady
Because I know that's what you needed to see and hear
As you lay in the hospital bed for one last night
Before the monitors and tubes took your final breath from me.
Often times I wonder why the writers decided to put me on two knees
Crying in the bleak midwinter at the foot of your grave
Before I could ever bend down on one.

Music

Prelude

As the hammers gently pounded on the coiled strings inside the hollow wooden body of the grand caravan of tears, serenity, and dance, my mind gradually shielded my closed eyes from the blinding light casting its magnificent luminescence onto me. As my vision transcended to a plane of ease and placid tranquility, my body achieved supreme sentience and blended with my soul to guide my fingers as they danced across the ivory platforms, waltzing to Allemandes and Sarabandes with calculated precision and gleeful color. My heart surfed the ripples of crescendos and arpeggiated chords until the swells collapsed gracefully onto the shore as the applause erupted to my right, transporting me back onto that stage, seated on a solitary bench staring down at a pristine grand Steinway. I calmly took my hands off the keys and placed them on my lap momentarily before standing up and turning to face the audience. Their ovation continued to roar as my eyes adjusted to the spotlight and could begin to make out thousands of beaming faces. Painted on each countenance was an expression of different realities and stories begging to be told and heard. I captured the emotional details of each face in my head as I took a bow and walked off stage and into the private confines of darkness.

For as long as I've been a pianist, I never grew comfortable with the end of a performance. It wasn't nerves or the prospect of performing at large concert venues seating thousands in grand auditoriums. I become far too engrossed in the music and its magnetic orbit to preoccupy myself with the sea of peering eyes attentively piercing gentle daggers at my every move. No, it's the finality of it all. Those few seconds wherein there's nothing left to do. The audience has nothing to anticipate. As I relax my muscles and remove my hands from the keys, the spectators too ease their heightened tension and allow themselves to sink back slowly into their seats, exerting a sigh of relief shared by everyone in the room. It's as if the journey we're all endeavoring is suspended indefinitely and all the healing that comes with it just stops. I earnestly wish I could tirelessly and continuously play the world's stories out loud for eternity but I am simply mortal.

My name is Ayana. I was born 17 years ago in *Modena, Italia* to a Somali refugee and an Italian schoolteacher. *Mio padre* escaped from the east African coast as a child when he lost his parents in the crossfire of a rebel offensive siege near his hometown. Both parents were killed instantly when a car bomb spontaneously exploded just three meters away while they were returning home from the market on a Saturday afternoon. He stowed away as a young boy onto a merchant ship heading to Europe and found himself at the port of *Palermo* in *Sicily*. He worked at the docks, learning Italian from the travelers coming to and from the port, until he had saved enough money to sail across the Tyrrhenian and reach *Livorno*. One of his first jobs there brought him to *Firenze* where he met *mia madre*, an arts student at *l'Università degli Studi di Firenze*. My father immediately relocated to *San Niccolò*, just south of the city center, until my mother finished her studies.

The two of them fell madly and passionately in love during my mother's final two years at university. My father found work as a *cuoco* at a local restaurant and would learn new recipes to cook for my mother every evening after she finished her classes. She would write him letters and poems that he would bring to work every morning. He'd read those beautiful notes about how much my mother missed him and how excited she was for his latest culinary creations and he became consumed with one thought: spending the rest of his life with her. He pushed himself to improve his skills in the kitchen rapidly and eventually became the *capo cuoco* at his restaurant. A month before my mother's graduation, he received an invitation from a friend to open a restaurant together in *Modena*, a surprise he shared with my mother at her ceremony. The two of them moved to *Firenze* together for two years afterwards until my father finally had enough money to co-finance the restaurant. They got married right before leaving for *Modena* to begin the rest of their lives.

I was born into an unstable and heartbreaking world. Decades of unfettered climate change had turned the world's natural disasters into apocalyptic nightmares with increasing recurrence. Governments, strained by the economic and infrastructural damages from earthquakes, hurricanes, fires, and the like, were toppling like dominoes across the globe. Militant groups seized the opportunity to launch violent rebellions and wars had become too innumerable to count and keep track of. Every passing day was another tick on a time bomb of catastrophe and loss of human life.

However, I was also born out of opportunity. A few months before giving birth to me, my mother was offered a prestigious job to teach at a local magnate school the upcoming school year. It was a monumental opportunity for her because she had struggled to find consistent work in *Modena* after moving with my father. They were stressed about having a child with only a single source of income but were more than relieved when my mother received the phone call from *il preside*. It was because of this that my father would constantly refer to me as his *raggio di sole*. My parents truly believed that I was a blessing in their lives and that good fortunes were forthcoming for our family.

Growing up, it was difficult to avoid the glaring headlines circulating throughout the news cycle every day. Morbid descriptions about atrocities committed by both government backed military forces and rebel groups. Death tolls from typhoons in Asia. Terrorist threats in America. Refugee crises and exoduses in Africa. Financial meltdowns all across Europe and South America. Keeping up with the numbers and statistics from each seemingly disjoint *tragedia* was exhausting. Even more so was reading the stories saturated with horror and sadness that emerged from each humanitarian disaster. Our world was falling apart at the seams and its current trajectory was aimed straight at absolute destruction. As a young *bambina*, I was sheltered somewhat from the morbidity and overall weight of it all by my parents who protected me from the melancholy encroaching into our lives. My parents wanted nothing more than for me to be happy and enjoy the splendors of our quiet town while the rest of the world raged on in a gruesome war fueled by confusion and fear.

I took after my mother with my early interests in the arts, specifically music. My mother was more of a writer and painter than a musician, but she took pleasure in winding down in the evenings strumming her guitar and humming original melodies over simple chords. After dinner, she would sit me down on the floor and sing songs her parents had played for her when she was a child. I fondly remember my father walking through the door after closing up the restaurant downstairs and belting the lyrics *con spavalderia* in perfect harmony with my mother's gentle voice. She would smile so invigoratingly it filled our home with comfort and warmth. I looked forward to those performances each and every night, utterly mesmerized by the soothing therapy music brought to our *famiglia*. It was during those moments that I truly felt safe and content. My individual love for music eventually blossomed when my parents introduced me to the piano.

My father found an old upright piano that was horribly out of tune and my mother brought home some elementary books from her school to get me started. Almost instantaneously, I became immersed in learning my scales and arpeggios, ravenously studying music theory to form my fundamental basis so that I could begin playing more advanced songs. When I began lessons, my parents had to increase the duration and frequency of the lessons to allow my teacher to keep up with my progress. Eventually, I quit private sessions altogether and self-taught myself once I was self-sufficient in my ability to sight read and memorize pieces. I spent every waking moment at that piano, relentlessly building up my repertoire full of diverse sonatas and concertos and preludes and etudes and anything else I could find to play.

By the time I was eight years old, my father told me I was *un prodigio*. My face beamed with excitement when I heard those words. I was so proud of my accomplishments and knew that I wanted to play the piano for the rest of my life. Having my father acknowledge my hard work and talent provided me with validation that I was destined to share my performance with the world.

It was also around this time that my mother fell ill to a mysterious form of cancer in her *cuore*. *I dottori* were unable to conclusively determine the root cause and consequently could not offer my parents any guarantees of recovery. The cancer was discovered when my mother would occasionally suffer from sharp sweeping pains across her chest. She described the pain as *un impulso di fuoco ardente* in her heart that would bring her to her knees as she struggled to maintain her breath. The inflammation would last up to five minutes at a time and she would toe the delicate balance of consciousness all the while. Once the pain subsided, my mother would remain discombobulated and out of breath for a few minutes afterwards until her strength began to return. Although the painful outbursts seemed to be relatively few and far in between, each recurring episode weakened my mother significantly.

It absolutely devastated me to have to watch my mother endure such awful agony knowing I was utterly helpless in curing her illness. My father tried his hardest to remain optimistic as the months continued to pass with no cure or positive developments. He didn't want my mother's pain to consume me collaterally; I was just a child and needed to live a normal life. But how could I? I had never known darkness before because there was always light in her eyes and comfort in her arms. This woman was the foundation that kept our home rooted and centered. She was a *supereroina* who shielded me from the world's evil.

I was angry. Infuriated. Why did God decide to curse this pure angel who held nothing but unconditional love in her heart for *sua figlia, suo marito, i suoi studenti,* and every one of His earthly creations? Wasn't there enough to smite and cast divine judgment upon in His forsaken damnation? *Perché Dio stave uccidendo mia madre? Qual è stato il motivo?* How was this fair? I screamed these questions silently in my mind every night as I cried myself to sleep, unable to fathom the indiscriminate cruelty of my God.

The restless nights and emotional weight of seeing my mother suffer caused me to spiral into a reclusive depression. I stopped attending school completely and locked myself in my bedroom, only escaping my confinement to briefly check in on my mother until the sight of her youthful frailty brought tears to my already reddened eyes and forced me back into hibernation. Sometimes when I lay awake in my bed in the dead of night I could hear my father's soft sobs in the kitchen. His quiet crying crept silently next to me and wrapped its sorrowful arms around my small body, temporarily silencing my rampant thoughts so I could sleep. My father's tears pushed my grief to seek companionship with ire: the same ire which consumed my heart when *i dottori* delivered the cancer diagnosis to us in the hospital.

My father wearily returned home from the restaurant one evening to a gargantuan pile of smashed wood and shattered ivory littered with broken steel springs spilling across the living room floor. His daughter sat on the ground in the center of the mess, hammer in hand, *sangue* streaming down her palms, sobbing incessantly. In a fit of sweltering rage, I found one of my father's hammers in his toolbox and stood face to face with the piano, glaring at its worn keys and roughened wood exterior. As tears began running down my face, I started swinging the hammer uncontrollably at the worthless piece of junk standing in front of me. For years, I spent so much time glued to the bench pounding away powerfully and gracefully on the keys, pouring *mia anima* into the notes on the sheet music and ignoring everything happening around me. For years, I wasted so much time mastering an art that served no purpose and was merely a stupid hobby. What could a piano do to help my mother? I was scared and lost and unable to properly process my emotions. So, I just swung and swung until I collapsed onto the floor, my hands battered and bleeding from pointed wood and ivory shards.

I sat there for maybe an hour before my father arrived. I felt his arms cover me in a gentle but firm embrace and suddenly I was crumbling. Every inch of my body lost its hold on the physical world and melted away into a pool of despair and weakness. My fingers relaxed and the hammer slipped out of my hands, hitting the floor with a deafening rattle next to my foot.

"Careful, you'll get hurt, darling. Your hands are already bleeding."

I looked down at my bloodied hands in dismay as the reality of my actions set in. The numbness disappeared and the searing pain cutting through my hand was all I could think about. My eyes glanced around the room at the carnage surrounding me and I felt nothing but relief. I silently and subconsciously made *un patto* with myself that day to never touch that damned instrument again, only focusing on helping my mother recover and survive. My father officially withdrew me from school and I began an independent study program at home. This allowed me to help out at the restaurant which saved my father some money. Sometimes, I would sneak off with some leftovers during lunch and raced to my old school on my bike with pasta and desserts stuffed into my backpack. My friends and former classmates would meet me at the back fence on the playground to purchase meals from the restaurant. It was easy to accumulate demand from the schoolchildren because I distinctly remember how horrendous the lunches were. These kids were truly blessed to have me sell them my father's dishes.

As a family, we struggled to keep up with my mother's increasingly frequent hospital visits. The list of medications continued to grow and so did the intensity of her treatments. Technically, my mother was still receiving half her annual salary in disability pay two years after leaving her job at the magnate school. The governing board, out of sheer kindness, decided to continue paying her to help us with the medical costs. We were extremely grateful because if not for my mother's disability pay, my father and I would have fallen too far behind on expenses to refill prescriptions and continue treatments for my mother.

Moreover, it appeared that the world was beginning to recover from years of conflict and carnage. Buoyed by a rejuvenated economy and significant improvements to the weather cycle, my father's restaurant began welcoming more guests than he ever had in years prior. This meant that I would have to work longer hours and work much harder to attain the extra income from my lunch time schoolyard sales so our family could continue paying the bills and staying in the only home I'd ever known. The rough hours paired with mounting schoolwork felt lightened by the overall sense of positivity and replenished will in our surrounding community. It seemed as though people were becoming increasingly *ottimista* about the future of our world.

The summers were noticeably cooler and storms were primarily reduced to healthy bouts of rain that boosted the local agricultural output greatly. Dry spells in the hills appeared to cease and the consequential wildfires became a worry of the past. As governments around the world began to recover their authority and control over their respective countries' fiscal and environmental infrastructures, violent uprisings subsided over peaceful negotiations and thorough reform. I remember feeling as if the world's rotation shifted and people had become much more symbiotic with a powerful pride in *solidarieta* as compared to the stark individualism that previously plagued our world's *umanità*.

By the time I was 14, my father's business had recovered exceptionally well and his restaurant was actually able to expand its operations and supply chain network. He convinced his old friend to accept investors' money to open up another location across town with each of them operating one restaurant individually. My father hired on more staff and even afforded a manager to help run the restaurant on a day to day basis, leaving my father with more time to spend taking care of my mother and helping me with my studies. That new reality was a breathtaking change of pace from what we had previously become accustomed to and I cherished those blissful times to this day.

On a hazy Saturday evening that same summer, after a long day of handling deliveries and taking inventory of ingredients in the hot, claustrophobic rear of the restaurant, I was treated to a special, intimate dinner with my father in the kitchen of his restaurant. I had only been allowed into the kitchen a couple times before, and even then, I was merely running through in a hurry while working. But that evening my father had a small table set up in the center and when I walked in I saw that all the cooks had already finished for the day and everything was wiped down and cleaned thoroughly.

"Hello, darling. Sit with me. I made your favorite for dinner: *Conchiglie Ripiene al Forno.*"

Baked stuffed shells. Growing up, my mother would bake these wonderful jumbo shells stuffed neatly with ricotta cream, mozzarella, and marinara, topped with a touch of parmesan. This was quintessential of one of our weekend dinners and I always looked forward to helping her stuff the shells in the kitchen. It had been a very long time since my mother last prepared a meal for the family: her health prevents her from doing so. I began to tear up while staring at my plate as my eyes caught the attention to detail my father put into replicating my mother's old recipe.

The aroma of melted cheese blended with the sweet tanginess of the marinara swam up through my nostrils and settled right in the center of my heart. The edges of the shells were golden, only slightly different in texture from the rest of the pasta: just how I liked them. Perched on top of the stuffing was an infusion of speckled white melted parmesan and thinly sliced parsley. It was truly a magnificent and hungering spectacle to take in.

"Thanks, Dad. I haven't had these in years! What was the reason tonight?"

"Because I have some good news, honey."

Una vacanza! My father had been planning and organizing a trip for the two of us over the past few weeks while we were working long days and even longer nights to make ends meet. An effervescent wave of excitement poured out of me as I jumped up and hugged my father. While my squeals of happiness echoed throughout the empty kitchen, I felt scattered teardrops fall upon on my shoulder as my father's hands pulled me in tighter.

"I don't want to leave your mother here, but she wants us to go."

The emotions of the moment turned somber quickly as my thoughts ventured away from the elation I had felt before. My father had been working ceaselessly for years now to ensure that our family would not fall apart as my mother's illness only continued to worsen. Yet, he felt guilty about planning a trip for the two of us: a much deserved trip for him.

I realized then that it was my father's undying commitment to and love for my mother that ultimately kept us pushing and drove us forward all this time. Their adoration and perpetual desire to uplift and protect one another was something I had always marveled at. They both taught me at a very young age that love has the power to transcend even the most daunting forces that sweep through our lives unannounced, solely intent on wreaking havoc and destruction. A love I had only ever remotely came close to feeling once: with music during my adolescence.

My father and I left for the *Costiera Amalfitana* a few months later with heavy hearts and mindful optimism. This vacation served as a reminder that we deserved to reward ourselves and enjoy our lives even when it seemed as though our world refused to give us a break. Before leaving, my father hired a nurse to stay at home with my mother and take care of her while we were gone. Luckily, *la Costiera* was only a short flight away, although we tried our best to remain hopeful that no dire complications would arise in the next couple of weeks. I knew that one of my responsibilities during this trip would be making sure my father didn't worry too much and could actually relax and enjoy himself.

When we exited the airport taxi that drove us to our stay, my breath escaped my tired lips as I peered up at an astonishingly beautiful villa overlooking the cliffs by the Tyrrhenian.

"Dad, is this where we're staying?"

"Indeed, it is, sweetheart! Gio knows the owners

of the place and they are currently on holiday in France and let me rent the upstairs flat for a really good price. It's pretty nice, isn't it?"

"It's beautiful! I can't believe it. It looks right over the ocean!"

My father's face beamed with joy as he watched me jump up and down in the middle of the street as drivers angrily honked their horns at us to get out of the way. He knew all too well the feeling of a child's first holiday. While his first vacation was not nearly as glamorous as mine, he reveled in seeing the delight pour out of me as I ran towards the front door, dragging my suitcase at my feet. He had labored his entire life to create a life worth living not only for himself, but for his wife and especially his daughter. To be able to provide his family with even the most minimal luxuries he never could have dreamed of experiencing as a child was enough for him. And he had always been more than enough for me.

I spent that first afternoon aimlessly skipping around the villa, exploring each and every corner of the house and rummaging through the cabinets and drawers as the warm sun began to lower overhead, casting luminescent rays through the many open windows. There was so much to discover and the decorations blended the overall splendor of it all together. Never had

I been in such a gargantuan mansion with so many luxurious ornaments and features.

I felt like the main character in a movie. There were *faretti* all over me as I danced in my bedroom to an imaginary soundtrack playing in my head. The scene was set in a bustling beach town filled with shops and restaurants, neighbored by other clusters of quiet, lazy towns. A cool sea breeze wiped away the blistering late summer heat as crowds of locals and tourists marched down onto the white sand beaches, towels in hand, ready to relax and enjoy the sun. Children splashed each other playfully near the shoreline as sailors and surfers caught rippling waves further out. And there I sat, perched by the windowsill in my room, observing the overwhelming feeling of calm and tranquility beneath me.

"Ayana, come downstairs! We're leaving for dinner soon and I want to take you around town!"
"Coming!"

My father and I walked through the winding streets, losing ourselves in the maze of souvenir shops selling shirts and trinkets, food stands offering delicious smelling snacks, and a bevy of small restaurants leaking a collectively mesmerizing aura of traditional Italian cuisine. The narrow alleys were filled with clamoring patrons excitedly weaving through the stores, impatiently shopping for gifts and finalizing dinner plans. I knew we couldn't afford to indulge quite like the other tourists but I took solace in imagining myself in their shoes. Being able to make impulsive purchases while on holiday was a dream I found worth living for. At the same time, strolling through a new city with my father while relieved of the constant stress and worries back home was surely a blessing.

I spent my days passing through different pockets of life and wonder along *la Costiera*, soaking in the warm sun, and taking the ferry to and from *Capri*. In the evenings, my father took me to a different restaurant each night for dinner and I couldn't have been happier tasting such splendid recipes. Sometimes I wondered if the entire purpose of the holiday was for my father to expand his menu. He always seemed so intently focused on the dishes served to him everywhere we dined. Maybe he just wasn't able to stop being *il cuoco* even when traveling. Whatever the case may be, I was pleased to see him actually enjoying himself and allowing himself to truly rest. It warmed my heart that we could experience such wonderful moments together.

"Honey. Wake up. Ayana, please wake up."

My eyes struggled to open with no light in the

room to assist. I could barely make out the shape of my father hovering over my bedside with his arm on my shoulder.

"Yes, Papa? What time is it?"

"It's still very early, dear. I'm sorry but we have to leave. Right now."

After a few seconds of adjusting to the darkness, I could see my father shaking. His voice wavered as he tried to get me out of bed to pack up my belongings.

"Dad, what's wrong? Why are we leaving? You said we were leaving on Sunday!"

"Your mother has had another episode… this one worse than the others. I just got off the phone with the nurse before I came in. I need to go see her immediately."

My mind spun into a deep spiral, plunging furiously down through *un vortice* of emotions and confusion. My initial grief sputtered off and gave way to an overwhelming rush of guilt. I felt ashamed that I hadn't been thinking about my mother and her ailing health. I tried to think back to the last time I checked in on her and couldn't even remember. Had I become too engrossed in my own blessings that I neglected my mother's misfortune? Was it selfish of me to dispel my inhibitions while my mother couldn't? My heart sunk to my stomach as my emotions continued to unravel into the dark void of my room. I stopped packing abruptly and sat down on my bed, curling my legs up to my chest in a ball and began sobbing incessantly. My father heard me crying from his room and came running over to join me on my bed. He gently wrapped his arms around me and together we shared another moment: one of *rimorso, tristezza,* and *angoscia*.

I alternated between restless sleep and somber contemplation as my anxiety kept me company throughout the train ride back to *Modena*. Across from me, my father remained steadfastly awake the entire time as he stared out the window with deep concern. I wondered what he was thinking about. I wondered if he was blaming himself for leaving my mother at home while he went on a vacation. While he sat there unmoving and stoic, I hoped my guilt was enough for the two of us because my father was truly not to blame. If I hadn't been so excited to leave our life behind, even for a couple weeks, neither of us would have been in this situation.

When we arrived back home, I sprinted out of the taxi, through the restaurant, and upstairs towards the front door of our house, leaving my father behind with all our luggage. My heart immediately plummeted through the foundations in the floor when I caught sight of my mother in the living room. The nurse motioned to me to be quiet as my mother was sound asleep on the sofa. My legs buckled beneath me as I began shaking uncontrollably, staring at her softly breathing body. She looked immensely *debole*, ghastly even. Her skin was noticeably paler than I remembered and her breaths much more uneven and ragged than before. I heard a couple of loud thuds behind me as my father's boots announced themselves through the doorway.

"Oh, my God. Chiara. I'm so sorry, dear."

He rushed over to her side and sat down gently beside her, wrapping his arms slowly over and around her. He began sobbing quietly into her shoulder while his eyes closed and body tensed. Eventually, my father looked up at our nurse to ask her a question:

"How long has she been asleep for? Can I wake her?"

"Yes, go ahead. She's been asleep for a couple hours now. She seems to be doing better this morning than last night. I think it'll be okay for her to wake up."

"Chiara wake up. Please, darling. Wake up."

My father lightly shook my mother's arms while still holding her and brushed her delicate hair from her face. He continued pleading into the air of our living room but my mother was unresponsive. Desperation flushed through my father's veins as he grabbed her tighter and raised his strained voice.

"Chiara, please! I need you to wake up right now! I need to know you're okay, my love."

Not wanting to cry in front of our nurse, I leapt to my feet and ran to my room. I crashed and tumbled into bed and began sobbing violently into my pillow. *Mia madre stave morendo proprio di fronte a me?* I refused to believe that my mother could die without speaking to me one last time. I refused to believe she wouldn't be able to see me graduate school. Or go to college and get married. I needed her to meet her grandchildren. Sing and play with them like she did with me. And dance with my father one last time before they get too old and weak. There was simply too much left unwritten in her story for this day to be the final chapter. My tears gradually began singing a lullaby to put me to sleep after such an emotionally heightened day and the remnants of my grief agreed to a ceasefire with my anxiety to let me rest.

I slept through the rest of the day and awoke at nighttime. Through the darkness, I stumbled to my bedroom door and cautiously walked out towards the living room, apprehensive about what sight awaited me. As my vision caught up to my footsteps, I could make out a faint light breaking through the absolute darkness. My mother lay still on the couch where she was hours prior, silently breathing as our nurse sat in a nearby chair sound asleep with just a single small lamp illuminating the room. I stopped a few feet away from my mother and watched her sternly. My body refused to will itself to move any further yet I wanted so badly to lie down next to her. There existed a stubborn disbelief trying its absolute hardest to manifest reality in my mind that we were turning the penultimate corner in my mother's life. The wells in my swollen eyes had dried but my lip trembled sporadically as I watched my mother burn through her reserve tanks with every wistful breath.

Although I had dedicated my entire life to helping my father take care of my mother, there had always been a predilected injunction in our timelines where a certain devastation awaited. A patient harbinger of *tragedia* lurking in the shadows of our minds until the opportune moment to feast on the inconvenience of time. Its claws had already begun to scratch and tear their way through the fabric of our lives and now *la bestia* all but smelled blood in every direction. With its presence came an inescapable sense of helplessness that I blamed on myself every day. The closer this monster came, the more inflammatory my self-deprecation and limitless indictment became.

I felt pathetic. Weak, even. I would walk barefoot through impassable terrain and move the steepest of mountain ranges and wade through a torrential downpour and bear the weight of the world on my shoulders to rid my mother of her eternal suffering. But when I face *l'occhio del ciclone* my arms are limp, my legs brittle, and my mind numbed. I found that in the direst moments I could only will myself to cry but my tears are not magic. They were not medicine. They did little to relieve my pain and they did nothing to give my mother the strength she so desperately needed to live.

Two weeks passed which felt like one long, arduous blur of a day. My mother shifted in and out of her continuous state of unconsciousness only to open her eyes blankly at the world for a quick moment, incognizant of her surroundings, and return to sleep. My father spoke less and less when he was at home. Our nurse remained optimistic but often times it appeared even she didn't believe her own words of encouragement. I kept to myself studying in my room and only left to help my father at the restaurant or pick up groceries from the market. I would check in on my mother briefly each day to make sure she was still alive and breathing but beyond that I didn't have the courage to watch her beautiful *anima* wither away.

One Saturday morning, I awoke to a hazy sunray streaking through the window near my bedside. As I yawned and took in the fresh morning air, I heard the sound of something heavy being dragged across the living room floor. The wood screeched with every inch pulled and the dissonant marcato of the blaring clamor startled me wide awake. I jumped out of bed and quickly marched into the living room to see what the source of the disturbance was. As soon as I entered the room I stopped in my tracks and stared, my mouth agape and frozen in awe, at the breathtaking black Bechstein baby grand piano sitting in the corner.

After setting the brakes on the wheels of the piano, my father looked up at me with a shaking, exhausted smile.

"Good morning, sweetheart. Surprise."

I could tell there was pure joy in his sentiment but his aching voice belied his true emotions. Although there wasn't any noticeable excitement in his words, I knew he just wanted to return the long lost smile back to my face.

"What is this, Dad? Where did you get this from

and why?"

"Your mother woke up this morning while I was heading down to work and told me she missed hearing you play the piano. So, I called a friend of mine who owns a music store and he sold me this one at a major discount. I hope you like it, Ayana."

I glanced over at the couch and saw my mother sitting upright smiling at me with tears in her eyes. I hadn't even noticed her until that moment and it took a few moments for my mind to process that my mother was awake and conscious.

"Oh my God, Mama you're up! I love you so much and I've missed you so much."

I ran to her and sat down gently beside her as we both began to cry. She slowly wrapped her arms around me as I leaned into her chest. Even in her frail and hollowed state, *il calore* exuding from her heart comforted me immensely.

"Oh, my dear child. How I've longed to hold you again. Would you please sit down and play my favorite Sonata for me? I haven't heard you play in years..."

Looking up at the piano across the room from me, I felt my body tense up as my mind embarked on a dizzying journey through nostalgic highways with turbulent emotional winds. Its pristine ivory keys shone in the delicate manner with which they were crafted as the finish on the wood reflected the sunlight poking through the living room. Without any thought, I lifted myself off the couch and slowly wandered over to the bench as if the Bechstein had placed a magnetic allure on my heart. Before I knew it, I was sitting down facing the piano with my hands placed in position to begin the lower octave C Major arpeggio that opens up the third movement of Beethoven's Sonata No. 21.

It was as if I had been possessed by the young girl who lived and breathed the notes on the sheet music and knew nothing *di angoscia o dolore o sofferenza o cinismo* towards the world around her. The bright eyed and impassioned girl who internalized every ounce of her parents' otherworldly love for her and reciprocated it as best she could: pouring her *anima* into the magnificent chords that rained down on the rapidly ascending and descending harmony as the two hands alternated singing to one another. I hadn't touched a piano in years but my fingers and my mind never let go of their firm grasp on the keys.

An out of body experience like no other, I felt as if I was watching my hands from above surf over the keys with meticulous precision and graceful *poesia* through a mind of their own. Just as soon as it started, the song ended. Ten minutes had passed and I hadn't even noticed. I returned to my body and stared down at my shaking fingers intently. How did I manage to do that? There was a deafening silence in the room where just moments before a bevy of arpeggios and trills saturated the airwaves. A significant part of me was too scared to look up and face my parents. Was it bad? Did I black out and just sit there staring at my hands the entire time? With no recollection of my performance I gradually lifted my eyes off the keys and up at my father while keeping my head lowered.

There was a rejuvenated smile adorning his face along with some dried tears on his cheeks. He stood motionless and communicated through his eyes the absolute state of shock he was in. He looked younger.

"Ayana… I'm speechless. You truly are an incredible girl. How lucky we are that we've gotten to hear you play such delightful music all these years. My one of a kind daughter."

Equal parts pride and joy beamed from my father's words and flew straight into my heart. A sense of calm and belonging began to course through my veins and I was immediately transported back in time to when I was 10 years old and at the peak of my prodigious career as a pianist.

Life in my house was much more serene then. The world around us was trapped in a seemingly endless cycle of chaos but confined in the safety of these walls, I was able to focus on piano, my mother was still teaching her classes, and my father didn't have to break his back every day trying to hold everything together for us. Oh, how things changed so quickly for the worse for our family. Sometimes it felt as if we were *maledetti* or being *punito* for something unbeknownst to us. My mother's health progressively declined more rapidly just as the rest of the world seemed to be recovering from decades of grueling conflict and destruction. Was my mother some sort of sacrifice for everybody else on Earth? How was that fair at all? It upset me to ponder the possibility that someone as selfless and undeserving as my mother could be responsible for bearing everyone's suffering at once.

Snapping back to reality, I returned my father's praise with a shy smile and calmly stepped away from the piano, turning towards the sofa. The elation I saw on my mother's face gave me butterflies. She let out a gleeful laugh that echoed through the room. One that none of us had heard in a terribly long time. One that caused me to collapse to the ground in an emotional panic. The very sound of my mother's silly laughter was what I had clung to firmly whenever I was scared as a young child and hearing it again after all these years, I didn't know how to react.

"That was just fantastic, Ayana. Thank you. I already feel so much better after hearing you play again. Please never stop doing what you love. It brings me such joy to see you back sitting in front of a piano after so many years. It really is where you belong, my child."

She wasn't lying. Her face seemingly restored some of its lost color and her energetic voice exuded newfound strength. It warmed my heart to see my music invigorate my mother as such and I wanted nothing more than to continue to make her happy. I quickly realized that my self-deprecation and self-pity was completely unwarranted. My frustration with my failure to physically produce *una cura* for my mother led me to abandon a source of contentment for not only my mother but myself as well. Destroying our family's piano and stubbornly deciding to never play again robbed me of my love for music and my mother's opportunities to distract herself from her treatments and everlasting pain. It turned out to be a much more selfish act than selfless, regardless of how much I was able to help out over the last few years.

Suddenly, I heard the soft pitter patter of

raindrops falling on our house and looked outside the window to see that the sun had disappeared and a light drizzle had begun. It was quite a beautiful instance of spontaneity. Our living room dimmed into a somber gloom but the simultaneous peace and serenity filling the ambience comforted each and every one of us. My father stood at the foot of the piano with his arms crossed staring lazily at the racing waterdrops on the window while our nurse closed her eyes and snuck in some much needed rest. I made my way to the couch next to my mother and we remained still in a seemingly endless embrace as the rain continued to trickle down. That moment remained engrained in my heart throughout the coming years as our lives had begun to change forever, again.

L'autunno came that year rather demonstratively with sporadic bouts of heavy rainfall and cold, windy nights. It almost seemed as if *l'estate* instantaneously disappeared that first day I returned to the piano. Life more or less returned to normal with my father working long nights at the restaurant while I continued to help him when I took breaks from studying and practicing piano. My mother's condition reverberated between swells of *vitalità* and *fragilità*. Whenever I noticed she was in a particularly weak state, I would head over to the piano and play her a few of her favorite songs. If she was awake, she'd always smile at me and thank me for cheering her up. I cherished possessing the ability to redirect my mother's fortunes at a moment's notice and it filled me with immeasurable warmth to see her visibly happy so often. Once the trees were stripped bare of their colorful autumn leaves, we had finally become fully settled into our new normal. After months passed with no extreme health scares, my mother no longer required the constant supervision of a nurse. With the weather becoming much colder and stormier, I spent increasingly more of my time inside the house and helped my mother whenever she needed me to. *L'inverno* that year brought the first *nevicata* I had ever experienced in my life. However, it didn't come as a gentle overnight *miracolo* I'd wake up to one weekend morning. The global temperatures had become so extremely cold that year that what was forecast as dangerously heavy rainfall a week before Christmas turned out to be a blistering *tempesta di neve* that tore through the north of *Italia*.

The week-long blizzard continued beyond Christmas, preventing anybody in town from leaving their homes. Forced to close his restaurant down, my father was able to spend his days taking care of my mother. That year we weren't able to buy presents for each other so my father and I put on *un concerto* for my mother instead. We practiced songs while she slept, sometimes during the day when she took naps and late at night after we were certain she was asleep. I had learned a bevy of new songs and even learned some specifically for Christmas. While I practiced piano, my father taught himself basic chords on my mother's old guitar. I greatly admired my father's dedication to learning the guitar for my mother's entertainment.

"I want to do something special for your mom this year. I know how much she misses playing guitar, especially for you, and I think this will be something fun for the two of us to do together as well."

There truly was nothing that this man wouldn't do for my mother and he proved it time and time again. I've witnessed it my entire life, yet he continues to surprise me with his unending thoughtfulness.

When Christmas evening rolled around, the three of us gathered in the living room by the fireplace and after drinking some hot cocoa and telling stories, my father told my mother to close her eyes as the two of us quietly got up to prepare for our show. I sat down at the piano while my father grabbed my mother's guitar and pulled a stool from the kitchen into the room. He looked over at me nervously and revealed a childish smirk. He counted down from three with his fingers and began lightly strumming the guitar. We opened our playlist with *Gesù bambino*, to which my mother immediately opened her eyes and chuckled. As father and daughter played and sang in unison, my mother lightly whispered the words under her breath.

"You guys are ridiculous! When did you find the time to practice this? Do I really sleep that deeply? How did I not ever hear you guys?"

My mother laughed heartily in dismay as she sat back and watched us finish our little program. That night, as *Modena* submerged itself under a meter of snow, I fell in love with piano all over again. Being able to perform with my father for the first time, albeit only with my mother in the audience, was something I never thought would happen. I treasured that experience and clung onto the beaming glow radiating from my mother's face the entire time we were singing together for the rest of my life. In a life primarily remembered through a sum of moments, these were the ones I hoped to remember forever.

Our family was only given a short while to enjoy the holidays when *tragedia* struck. During the Christmas night storm, the electrical grid in the entire northern half of the country overloaded overnight. We woke up the next morning to a complete widespread power outage affecting half the nation. Unbeknownst to us and millions of other Italian citizens, a cyberterrorist organization seized the opportunity while our country slept to hijack control of the country's infrastructural operations, locking the government out of its own electrical systems. The outage prevented any of us from even being able to access the internet and thus, northern *Italia* was stranded digitally for hours before the government was able to broadcast an emergency message to our phones.

That same morning, on the other side of the world, armed insurgents launched a violent siege on the capital of Brazil in an attempt to overthrow the government. Although the two events were obviously not connected, their immaculate timing toppled the first of many dominoes due to fall after years of careful realignment. As our European neighbors struggled to help our government and its contracted power suppliers regain control of our electrical grid, the United States and its coalition of forces mobilized to help Brazil's military respond to what quickly became a multitude of rebellious attacks from several different factions, jostling for political and economic power in the region's most prosperous country.

We lived in our house through a seemingly eternal blackout for two more weeks before the Italian government was able to pay off the ransom to the terrorist organization and reestablish stable electricity to its citizens in the north. However, during that time, the conflict in Brazil had catastrophically expanded into an explosive war spread all throughout South America with hotspots in Brazil, Venezuela, Colombia, and Bolivia. The South American conflict dragged every world power into its vortex of death and displacement, leaving hundreds of millions of people around the globe affected in one way or another.

My father and I tried our best to distract my mother from the constant news updates concerning the war. She was so unapologetically empathetic to a fault that I knew her heart hurt for all the innocent lives either killed or ruined due to the widespread consequences stemming from the conflict. Her health was declining again and her medication could only suppress her pain for short periods of time. She refused to increase the intensity of her treatments without more optimistic opinions from the doctors concerning her chances of survival. The treatments were extremely exhausting and she reasoned that receiving them more often and having to endure the excruciating agony that followed wasn't worth it if there wasn't a positive correlation with recovery.

I found myself rapidly expanding my repertoire, seemingly learning a new song every day for my mother as her strength appeared to drain from her with each passing day. For a while, as she continued to struggle to fight against the aching in her chest, my mother still listened attentively as I serenaded her with a blend of etudes and contemporary ballads. After each song and performance her cheerful smile brought a tint of rosiness to her now pale cheeks and she'd thank me.

After my 15th birthday, however, she began falling asleep more often in the middle of my playing. Her energy dwindled dramatically from morning to midafternoon and my father began to struggle with a serious bout of depression. He was never able to see my mother awake as she tended to wake up after he left for work and would be sound asleep by the time he got home in the evenings. Every night before he trudged to his room to sleep, he would sit by my mother's side as she lay on the couch and talk to her, uncertain if she could hear a word he was saying but telling her stories about his days regardless. Sometimes I'd notice him sitting and talking to her for hours at a time until his body betrayed him and he'd catch himself falling asleep on her.

Watching my father perform the same ritual each and every night took its own separate toll on my mental health. Nothing either of us seemed to do was enough to help my mother continue her fight and we both feared she was gradually losing her will to live. I knew my mother wanted to be alive and be with her family for as long as she could but as the months passed, she remained increasingly stubborn about receiving extra treatment. The doctors had informed my father that they could not, in good faith, confirm that more intense treatment would help my mother feel any better; they could merely recommend it as something worth trying. This wasn't enough to convince my mother.

"I know my health has been getting worse and worse. I know you guys want me to listen to the doctors and change my treatment plan. But I need you guys to understand that I'd rather wake up every morning and be able to eat breakfast with Ayana, even if I can only finish half of it. I'd rather get to hear her play piano with a heart full of joy than to be barely conscious while her beautiful music plays out loud for nobody to hear. Do you understand?"

It absolutely and completely shattered my heart to have to accept that my mother's time was running out. When I was *una bambina*, I heard that a parent should never outlive their child. I never feared that could happen to my parents but what a cruel world this could be. Now, I was 16 years old wanting nothing more than to take my mother's place on that God forsaken sofa so that she could finally be rid of her torment. I would have gladly given up my own life for my mother to get back the last eight years of hers. It simply was not fair.

For the better part of the last year and a half or so, life has become eerily similar to the first eight years of my life. It has become almost impossible to keep track of the daily tragedies striking the world. China's economy crashed six months ago and the world is currently falling apart at the seams as a result. *La Guerra Sudamericana* has showed no signs of dying down and relations between nuclear powers have reverted to Cold War era levels of paranoia and distrust. Sea levels have risen at a historically fast pace as global temperatures increased beyond repair. The entire world is in utter and complete *caos*.

But life goes on, too. My father still runs his restaurant downstairs and business has actually been doing quite well for us. As counterintuitive as it sounds, with groceries becoming too expensive for individual consumers to purchase, the cheapest way to attain fresh food is in bulk wholesale and a restaurant is one of the best customers for such a supply chain. My father lowered his prices enough to a point where it became more cost efficient for the locals to dine at his restaurant more often than cooking at home. Strange, I know. But there has been nothing normal about our lives since the day I was born.

About a year ago, shortly after I turned 16, my

father found a brochure in the mail for a new music program opening up at the *Università di Bologna* not too far away. He encouraged me to apply as we hired our old nurse back to help take care of my mother. I auditioned and received my acceptance into the program about 9 months ago. Since then, I've been studying there four days out of the week and returning home on the weekends to see my family. Although I am just a first year student, I've advanced so rapidly through the curriculum that I've been invited to teach multiple masterclasses for older students as well as perform in the grand concert hall at some of the university's prestigious recitals.

Lately, however, my responsibilities at school have prevented me from being able to come home as often as I'd like. What used to be weekly visits have become biweekly or even once every three weeks. The last time I saw my mother, she was unconscious the entire weekend. Our nurse informed me that she hadn't been awake for over a week straight before I came home. When I wasn't sitting next to my mother on the couch quietly sobbing, I always found my way back to the piano. I'd play for hours, mindlessly embarking on a solitary journey across time periods and signatures until my aching fingers couldn't play any longer. Dejected and defeated, I'd return to my mother and eventually fall asleep quietly next to her. I swear I could feel her breaths becoming fuller and heavier after every exhausting session, which comforted me as I drifted away into a slumber.

Two weeks ago, I performed in a recital at school that was broadcasted on a local TV channel. My program was 30 minutes long and I spent the entire time pouring every emotion I harbored inside onto those keys, thinking about the last time I saw my mother at home. The way she lay there unmoving and barely showing any signs of life horrified and saddened me at the same time. Just as I had that late summer morning two years ago, I blacked out on the stage that night. When I returned to my senses, I found myself breathing heavily with my hands shaking while resting on the final notes I had just played moments before. I regained my composure eventually with a couple of deep breaths and gently eased my hands back onto my lap. Gradually, I raised myself off the bench and took two short steps to my right and looked up at the crowd in front of me. With the spotlight shining brightly on my face, I closed my eyes and took a bow.

When I got home that night, my father called me with some amazing news:

"Ayana, you were wonderful tonight! They were showing your performance on TV and your mother and I watched the entire thing! I am so proud of you, dear."

"Wait, Mom was awake to see me play? Has she been doing better?"

At that point, I didn't care about my performance in the slightest. I couldn't believe that my mother was able to see me play. She seemed so gravely ill and on the teetering edge of life itself last I saw her.

"Yes, honey. I started watching the beginning of it in the living room and after your first song ended I heard your mother shifting in her sleep. I turned over to her and her eyes started blinking slowly. I couldn't believe it either."

"Can I talk to her? Is she still awake?"

"Hello, Ayana. How are you my darling? You were fantastic up there tonight!"

I held in my tears as I sat on my bed in the darkness of my studio flat. The familiarity of my mother's voice appeared startlingly distant and foreign over the phone.

"I've missed your voice, Mama. It is so amazing to hear it again. Thank you, though. I'm so glad you guys got to hear me play, especially you."

"Every single time you sit down and play the piano, the world takes a backseat to your excellence, Ayana. Including the cancer in my heart. It has never been any match for you. My love for you will always prevail over anything that gets in its way. I want you to know that."

Her words and the familiar vigor in her voice that night have stuck in my head ever since. I've refused to allow my mind to forget and find myself replaying her beautiful words of affirmation in my head over and over again. Knowing my mother was able to wake up from her state of unconsciousness to see me play made me feel *potente*. Invincible, even. As if I wielded some profound weapon through my music that could pull her away from death when it neared.

Two weeks after that recital, I was scheduled to perform my first ever *concerto privato* at the university. Excited at such a grand opportunity to further my playing career, I called my father and asked if he would be able to attend, unsure if my mother was in good enough health to make the trip with him. He told me that she had been feeling much better ever since my most recent performance and said she wanted to come to *Bologna* and see me in concert. I was overjoyed and bought two tickets for them to attend.

Tonight was that recital. I spent all day pacing

around my flat, barely eating anything as I nervously and repeatedly checked the clock. It wasn't the prospect of performing for thousands of people who have come to see me play. It wasn't the fact that I was making history as the youngest student to ever perform a private concert at the university. It had been a month since I last saw my parents and I wanted tonight to be nothing short of perfect for them. My mother hasn't left the house in years, much less ventured outside of *Modena*. As I left my flat to head to the school, I decided I would dedicate my performance tonight to my parents.

I couldn't afford to purchase tickets in the front row for my parents but I knew which row they would be in. As I rehearsed on stage a few hours before the concert, I practiced glancing over in the general direction of their seats with the spotlight cast on me. I wanted them to be able to see my face and know that I was thinking of them while I was performing. I needed them to know how much I adored them and missed them. They were my whole life and nothing mattered more to me tonight than them.

In the blink of an eye, I was standing in the back corner of the stage in the darkness, staring down at my shoes. I could hear quiet voices emanating from the amphitheater ahead of me and focused my breathing to calm my nerves before hearing my name announced by the emcee. When I walked onto the stage from behind the curtains and made my way to the piano, I soaked in the blinding stage light fixated on me and allowed it to consume me. Once seated with my hands on the keys, I closed my eyes and exhaled a breath of relaxed relief. All the waiting from today was over and now I was ready to do the one thing I knew my whole life I was destined to do. I took one last look out into the crowd and inhaled one last breath before my hands took over and stole the show.

For an hour and a half, with the exception of a short intermission, I sat stationary on the bench and watched in amazement as my hands danced on the keys with perfect dynamic grace and astonishing power. As I neared the end of my performance, I felt a surge of emotion rush through my body from my heart outward. The ground started to shake beneath me as I concluded the final measures of Liszt's La campanella in G# Minor. I thought I heard the audience murmur as the tremors appeared to grow in size with every passing moment. Assuming it was merely my imagination and that I was having another out of body experience, I readied myself to conclude the concert with the final song: Rachmaninoff's Prelude in C# Minor.

I started off slowly as my hands started to pulsate with raw energy. No matter how much I tried to maintain the pace and slow build of the song's progressions, my hands were desperately seeking permission to execute a compelling show of strength. Struggling to contain the energy in my body, I succumbed to the heavenly light above me and released every ounce of strength I had. My hands pounded on the keys with such force I thought I was going to break a string inside the piano. As the song swelled and gained momentum, I heard terrified shrieks come from the audience. Rubble started to fall around me but I was unable to stop myself from playing. Painfully, I turned my head to see the destruction occurring in the concert hall.

Some people had gotten up and were running to the back doors to exit. Suddenly, the light no longer impeded my vision and I was able to see my parents sitting in the center of the room. They sat there motionless, my father with his arm around my mother, struggling to remain in his shaking seat. When I looked at my mother, my eyes were in disbelief.

She was healthy. Her face had completely restored its natural hue and her eyes no longer bore any resemblance to an abyss. There was life in her body and she looked remarkably younger. Tears were rapidly streaming down her face as she marveled at her daughter on stage.

Rachmaninoff's Prelude continued to manifest

itself into the open air while I tried my hardest to stop playing. As I sat there, unable to control my own possessed body, I began vehemently sobbing. With only a few lines left in the song, the concert hall was barely recognizable anymore. The roof had been torn off completely by a swirling gust of gale force winds. As the foundations of the building started collapsing all around me, I saw hundreds of people being crushed by large slabs of concrete. When the walls finally fell, I could see that the city of *Bologna* had become toppled to ashes. Fires and knocked down buildings stretched as far as the eye could see.

Elsewhere around the world, hurricanes spontaneously formed and made historically fast landfall on coastal regions. Devastating wildfires sparked out of nowhere in Africa and Australia. *La Guerra Sudamericana* had escalated immensely and immediately reduced the entire continent into a barren battlefield. America got cold feet and launched its nuclear missiles at both Russia and North Korea. All the other nuclear powers then responded promptly on both sides. With nuclear fallout now imminent, I noticed a gargantuan wall of water towering over 100 feet tall in the far distance to my left racing towards me, destroying everything in its wake. I looked at my parents one last time before my hands played their final c# minor chord and mouthed "I love you."

Alexttdo

Old Friend

I couldn't pinpoint the moment I met you
Or even the first time I saw you-
But it must have been special
Because for twenty three years now you've been my best friend.
I never quite understood my attachment to you.
But I took you everywhere with me:
School, vacation, car rides, all throughout the house.
Maybe you just made me feel comfortable.
Growing up, I couldn't shake the feeling that I was on an express
One-way trip to adulthood that zoomed on into the unknown
At blazing speeds too fast to recognize anything in the rearview.
There was always a reason for me to be more mature,
More intelligent, more put together,
More responsible, more grown up.
For someone who's always felt the youngest
In any classroom, office, or job,
You reminded me that it's okay to be young.
To be a child sometimes.
It's the unexplainable and immense spike in serotonin that floods my brain
When I come home from work and see your tiny little pink smile and blue pajamas.
It's the instant spread of warmth and comfort that resonates through my body
Whenever I pick you up and squeeze you into my chest.
As my days wither by and the problems begin to pile up insurmountably,
I ponder and fondly reminisce the simplicity of being a child
Sitting in my room playing with my teddy bear.

We would create fantastic adventures in my mind
That would take us to the furthest limits of the realm of imagination.
And some days as I lie awake in the dead of night
Dreading the rise of morning light,
I turn and grab you from the corner of my bed
And press you to my chest, closing my eyes and wishing things could be easier.

Author's Note

In lieu of the chapter introductions I wrote for "RED," I've decided to add some notes for the pieces in "BLUE" for added context and any explanations that may be needed. These notes will exclusively focus on the works of writing themselves rather than the topics chosen for the book. I hope you enjoyed reading "BLUE" and can't wait for you to read the books to come in the Colors series.

Loneliness

I wrote "deserving" very early on in 2019 while in the midst of working on "RED." I never intended to publish the poem as it was merely an impromptu illustration of my thoughts at the time. At my lowest, and consequently my depression's peak, I was a hollow, suicidal shell of myself. My desire to take my own life presented itself at the forefront of my mind multiple times a day and I'm thankful I never acted seriously enough on any of those whims. I had an unhealthy obsession with questioning my right to live my own life. So many wonderful blessings found their way to me and I couldn't understand why. At the time, I truly believed that there was nothing I had done in the 20 years and change prior to those days to deserve the amazing people and opportunities in front of me. The poem itself is quite the self-pity fest but very accurately portrayed my running thoughts at the time. I'd like to assure you that now I am in a much better place and have healed and grown tremendously since.

It took me much, much longer than I thought to get to a stable, healthy place in my own mind, however. This is when I was able to write "undeserving." I wrote "undeserving" in the middle of 2020 after I spent a little over a year stumbling through a bevy of changes in my life. It wasn't until my January trip to Japan that I truly began to understand my emotions and thoughts. By the end of my trip, I had written the first couple stanzas/paragraphs of "undeserving" and knew that it was going to be the response to "deserving." I realize that the time in between the two pieces is not made clear enough in the writing itself, so this note serves as a bridge between the two. For those of you that have been by my side from early 2019 until now, I hope you have been able to notice the change in my resolve and how much freer I have become because you've all played a very large part in it. Thank you.

Water

"Drowning" is a love letter of sorts to myself. As with most of my writing, I tried my hardest to veil who the poem is addressed to as best as I could and wanted it to appear like an ordinary heartbreak poem. For much of my life, I've struggled to love myself and have actually developed a seething self-hatred that so detrimentally harms my appreciation of the wonderful things I have felt and done in the past. The best way I can explain it is that I have always felt like there was a part of me that comes in and out of my life randomly that allows me to accept and love who I am but it never lasts long enough for me to develop a healthy relationship with my mind and soul. When that part of me is there within me, I feel invincible and fulfilled. But the earth shattering void it leaves behind when it disappears leads to the 'drowning' sensation I constantly feel.

As for the poem itself, the reading experience is intended to simulate physically drowning. The stanzas increase in wordiness and the run-ons by the end of the poem are pretty dramatically long. Once again, please enjoy the content of the poem and its reading experience without concern for my wellbeing. I am okay. Trust me.

Sleep

Oh, you know, just another love poem.

Emma's art for this topic is one of my favorites in the book. I asked her to make something that portrayed the different dreams in the poem and she delivered perfectly. The three dreams are beautifully drawn and overlayed on top of one another in such a nice way. You should definitely go check out her other illustrations and photography. They're amazing.

Sky

Oh look, another love poem. I had fun writing this poem because the movie metaphors just flowed so easily for me while writing it. Unfortunately, like most of this book, it's sad.

Music

Prelude is by far the most significant work of writing I have ever produced thus far in my career. It is both my longest and proudest single piece of writing and I hope you thoroughly enjoyed it. The idea and story for this novelette had been in my head for a long, long time. However, when I first started writing Prelude, I only thought of a barebones plot that required a lot of developing to get to where it is today.

I originally had an idea to write a simple story about a girl who plays an instrument with so much power she has the ability to help others while destroying something else simultaneously. With just that idea, I created Ayana and Prelude's complete storyline.

There's a lot I have to say about this story and my intentions behind certain thematic topics and messages. First and foremost, however, I want the reader to take away from the story whatever the reader initially thinks it is about. My writing is never intended to be unidirectional in meaning and that's partially the reason why it is seldom straight forward. With that being said, if you'd like to maintain your understanding of Prelude without my explanations, please skip the rest of this note. I don't want to ruin/alter your perception of the story without warrant!

My primary intention with Prelude was to explore our understanding and value of love. There are quite a few variations of love that are portrayed in the story: Ayana's parents' love for one another, Ayana's love for her parents and her family altogether, and Ayana's love for music/piano. I wanted the reader to think about how much we value these different kinds of love in our lives. The lengths Ayana goes to preserve and protect the love she feels in her life could be seen as extreme, but nothing she does is dramatically exaggerated in any way. I felt that her actions and motivations are organic and true to what we witness and feel in our daily lives. Although the story itself becomes quite supernatural by the end, the overwhelming majority of the story is very real and authentic to our modern day lives.

Moreover, the idea of blessings coming with a curse is weaved into the plot of the story. Every time Ayana seriously commits to playing piano, and as her skills develop more, the world around her suffers. Meanwhile, her mother is healed by her piano playing. This is indicative of her supernatural powers becoming stronger as she improves her piano playing. Ayana isn't aware of this until the very end when it's too late, but in her eyes, it was almost worth it. Although she doesn't want or intend to destroy the world just to save her mother, being able to see her mother healthy again was always at the forefront of her mind for more than half her life. In the end, she gets her wish but the ultimate curse comes to fruition as well.

Alexttdo

This little teddy bear is my oldest friend and he always puts a smile on my face. Don't question why he's named that. 2-year-old me was very creative. I wanted to end BLUE on a happy note so just look at him.

Also shout out to Emma for making him even cuter in her art than he is in real life which I had previously thought was impossible.